Froggy Went a Hopping

For Grandad with love - SM

First published 2007
Evans Brothers Limited
2A Portman Mansions
Chiltern Street
London W1U 6NR

British Library Cataloguing in Publication Data

Durant, Alan, 1958-
    Froggy went a-hopping. - (Spirals)
    1. Children's stories
    I. Title
    823.9'14[J]

ISBN-10: 0 237 53352 9 (hb)
ISBN-13: 978 0 237 53352 6 (hb)

ISBN-10: 0 237 5346 4 (pb)
ISBN-13: 978 0 237 53346 5 (pb)

Printed in China

Series Editor: Nick Turpin
Design: Robert Walster
Production: Jenny Mulvanny

Froggy Went a Hopping

Alan Durant
and Sue Mason

It was a fine bright day and Froggy was feeling very hoppy.

His fingers itched and his webby toes twitched.

He wanted to leap and hop and spring and sing.

But Froggy was all alone and he wanted the whole world to share his hoppiness.

So Froggy hopped off his lily pad and out into the big wide world.

Froggy hop hop hopped until he
came to some trees where birds
were singing. Twitter, twitter,
tweet, tweet!

Froggy's fingers itched
and his webby toes
twitched.

He was so very hoppy
he just had to sing too.

Croak, croak, ribbit!
Croak, croak, rib...

"Hey, frog!" a little bird
voice piped "You're ruining
our song. Hop it!"

"Sorry," croaked Froggy
and away he hopped.

Froggy hop hop hopped until he came to a meadow where bees swarmed in and out of flowers. Froggy's fingers itched and his webby toes twitched. He just had to join in. He poked his fingers into the flowers.

"Hey, that's our job, frog.
Leave those flowers alone!"
buzzed the bees angrily.
"Buzz off. Hop it!"

"Sorry," said Froggy and
away he hopped.

Froggy hop hop hopped to the top
of a hill where a band of bunnies was
jumping. Bounce, bounce, bounce!

Froggy's fingers itched and his webby
toes twitched.

He just had to bounce too.

But the bunnies were too fast and soon they had all bounced away.

Flop! Froggy was all alone … or was he?

"Hey frog!" snarled a voice behind him.

Froggy turned to see…

A fox! An angry mean grumpy old fox.

"You just caused my lunch to vanish," said the fox.

"Sorry," gulped Froggy.

"Well," said the fox. "I guess today I'll just have to eat Frog instead."

Froggy's fingers quivered
and his webby toes shivered.
The fox pounced ...
and Froggy leapt.

Up up above the bunnies, the bees and the birds, high high into the sky leapt Froggy until … flump!

He landed in the middle of a fluffy white cloud.

"Ooh," said Froggy as he looked down on the big wide world.

Night came. The sky darkened
and the stars came out.
Twinkle, twinkle, twinkle.

Froggy's fingers itched and his webby toes twitched.

He wanted to twinkle too.

But he couldn't.
Poor Froggy. Tears plopped
from his big bulgy eyes.

Suddenly thunder rumbled.
Lightning flashed.

Froggy's cloud turned black
and burst into raindrops.

Down
down
down fell Froggy down
down
down until …

Splash! He landed back in his very
own pond!

And there on his lily pad sat
another frog.

"Hurrah!" cried the frog. "It's such
a lovely wet night and I was feeling so
hoppy. I wished for someone to share
it with, and down you came like
a falling star."

"Oh," said Froggy.

Froggy's fingers itched and his webby toes twitched.

How very very hoppy he was.

Then Froggy and his new friend hop
hop hopped together all night long and
lived hoppily ever after.

Why not try reading a Spirals book?

Megan's Tick Tock Rocket by Andrew Fusek Peters,
Polly Peters, and Simona Dimitri
ISBN 978 0237 53342 7

Growl! by Vivian French and Tim Archbold
ISBN 978 0237 53345 8

John and the River Monster by Paul Harrison and Ian
Benfold Haywood
ISBN 978 0237 53344 1

Froggy Went a Hopping by Alan Durant and Sue Mason
ISBN 978 0237 53346 5